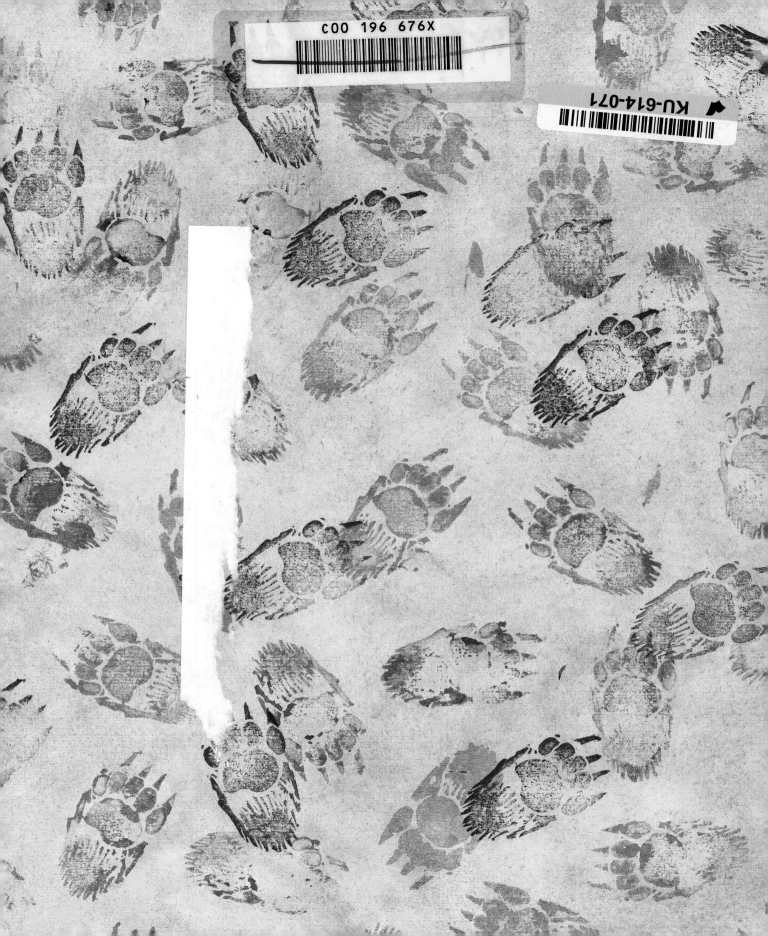

The rights of Ingrid and Dieter Schubert to be identified as the author and illustrator of this
work have been asserted by them in accordance with the Copyright, Designs and Patents Act, 1988.
First published in Great Britain in 1998 by Andersen Press Ltd., 20 Vauxhall Bridge Road, London SW1V 2SA.
Published in Australia by Random House Australia Pty., 20 Alfred Street, Milsons Point, Sydney, NSW 2061.
All rights reserved. Colour separated in Italy. Printed and bound in Belgium.
10   9   8   7   6   5   4   3   2   1
British Library Cataloguing in Publication Data available.
ISBN 0 86264 822 X
This book has been printed on acid-free paper

THERE'S A HOLE IN MY BUCKET

Ingrid and Dieter Schubert

Andersen Press • London

Bear was worried. The day was so hot, and the sun shone so fiercely, that the flowers in front of his cave were beginning to wilt. Their tired heads drooped and their leaves were limp.

"I must get them some water from the lake, at once ..."
said Bear to himself, "but what shall I carry it in?"

Bear went inside his cave to look.
He found a spoon — but that was too small.
He found a mug — but that wasn't big enough either.
He found a sieve — but that wouldn't carry *any* water,

because it was full of holes.
"I know," said Bear. "A bucket! I must have one somewhere."
And, sure enough, he found one, half hidden by an old box.

Bear set out towards the lake, but then he noticed something
bad about his bucket. There was a hole in it! What on earth
was he going to do now?

As he stood there, wondering what to do, Hedgehog came by. He was out for a stroll but he stopped when he saw Bear's gloomy face.

"Why so sad?" he asked.
"My flowers are thirsty," said Bear, "and I wanted to fetch
them some water from the lake. But I can't, because there's
a hole in my bucket."

Bear showed Hedgehog the bucket. Hedgehog saw the hole.
"You'll have to fix that hole," he said.
"With what?" asked Bear.
"With straw," said Hedgehog. "Come on, I'll help you gather it."

The two friends soon had plenty of straw but it was too long to use. Bear tried to break it but the straw was too tough. "You'll have to cut that straw," said Hedgehog.

"With what?" asked Bear.
"With scissors," said Hedgehog. "Wait here, I'll fetch some from my house."

While Bear waited, he watched the flowers drooping sadly in
the heat. He tried to cheer them up but it was no good.

At last, Hedgehog returned, carrying a large pair of scissors.
"Here you are," he said. "Now you can cut the straw."

Snip-snip, *snap-snap* went the scissors, but they wouldn't cut the straw.

"These are blunt!" said Bear, angrily. "Now what shall I do?"

"You'll have to sharpen those scissors," said Hedgehog.
"With what?" wailed Bear.
"With a stone," said Hedgehog. "Let's go and find one."

They searched and searched until they found a really good stone.

Then they carried it back to Bear's cave and Bear sat down to try and sharpen the scissors.

"Hold on!" cried Hedgehog. "That's not the way to sharpen scissors on a stone. It's too dry! You need to wet that stone!" "With what?" asked Bear. "With water!" said Hedgehog. "You'll have to get some from the lake."

"With what?" asked Bear, quietly.
"With a bucket!" replied Hedgehog.
"But there's a hole in my bucket," whispered Bear. "Now what?"
And this time, Hedgehog couldn't tell him.

As they both sat there not knowing what to do, it started to rain — softly, at first, but then harder and harder.
"Come on!" shouted Bear. "Into my cave! We can't stay here."

And while the rain poured down outside, Bear and Hedgehog had so much fun *in*side, that they quite forgot about their problem.

When the rain stopped, they went outside again — and what did they see? The flowers were nodding their heads and their leaves no longer hung limply at their sides. The rain had cheered them up! Bear was so pleased that he picked a huge bunch and gave it to Hedgehog.

"Because you were such a great help," he said.
Hedgehog was delighted. "Thank you, Bear. I shall go home and put them in water, at once!"
"That's a good idea," said Bear. "Do you have something to put them in?"

"Of course," said Hedgehog. "I must have a bucket somewhere!"

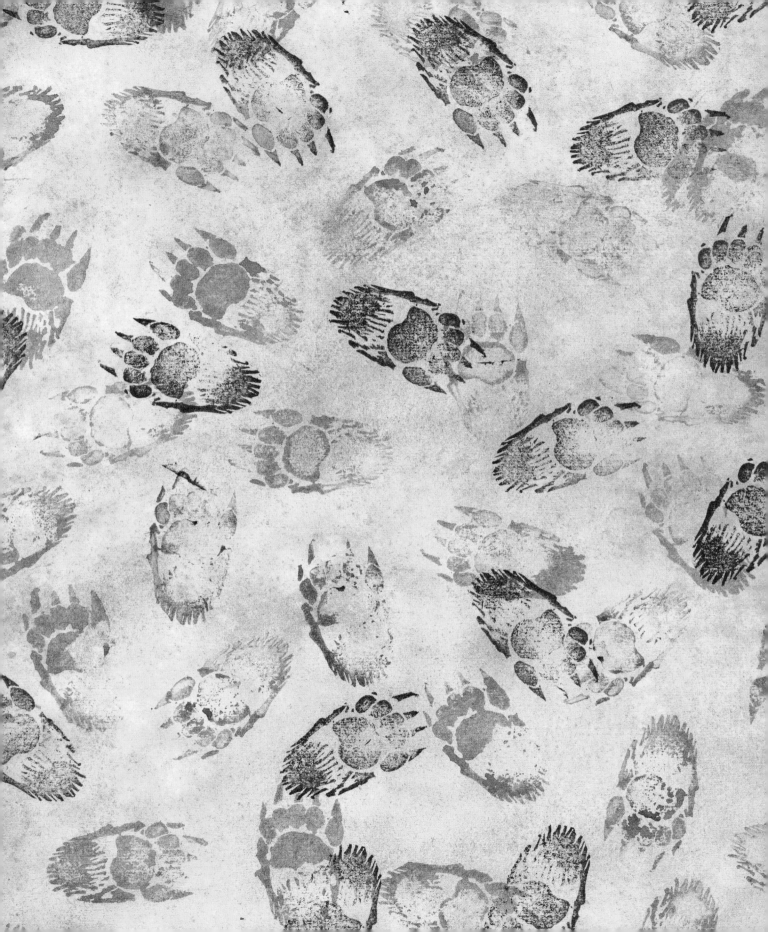